THE FATAL BODICE

by the same author

The Butcher
Lucie's Long Voyage

A L I N A   R E Y E S

The Fatal Bodice

translated from the French
by David Watson

Methuen

First published as *Au corset qui tue* in 1992
by Editions Gallimard, Paris

First published in Great Britain in 1993
by Methuen London
an imprint of Reed Consumer Books Ltd
Michelin House, 81 Fulham Road, London SW3 6RB
and Auckland, Melbourne, Singapore and Toronto

A CIP catalogue record for this book
is available from the British Library
ISBN 0 413 67950 0

Printed and bound in Great Britain
by Clays Ltd, St. Ives Plc

THE FATAL BODICE

What else is there but pleasure, when you've got a room, a window, and sunlight coming in? The pleasure of wallowing in inactivity, with languid daydreams flowing through your whole body . . . In the deep blue sky the plane stretches out its white tail, the willows on the lawn dangle their green hair.

I have taken my dress out of the wardrobe. So white. In bright light you have to squint to look at it. I carry it to the shaded part of the room, I see myself in the mirrors, walking with the dress by my side, I carry it as though I were holding it by the shoulder, I open the door of the wardrobe a little so that its mirror reflects my image in the wall mirror to infinity, myself in reverse, reverberating down a deep funnel of waves, a Russian doll smiling from the other side of endless sliding mirrors, with teeth like pearls.

My husband is such a wonderful lover. I put the dress away in a large cardboard box in the bottom of the wardrobe. I fold it carefully, it puffs up and sits quite nicely in its box, I feel like kissing it.

Under the ceiling I roll in the rectangle of sunlight. Sometimes he comes home and finds me there. Then he takes me, calls me his dove, his little butterpot, his well of love, well of night, do I know?

I think about him during the day. When the wind blows in the trees in the park and the leaves rustle I imagine that it is the soft cry of his body hair when I run my hand over it. 'Alice,' he whispers, and the branches of the poplars bow and dance, and curtsey wildly in the sky.

I often go to bed with some magazines he has brought me, some books, some food. I eat: marzipan. I look at: pictures in magazines. I read: novels in one go. I say: poems out loud. I get undressed, I see myself in the mirrors. I get out my white dress. I put it away. I feel cold, I get back into bed, pull the covers up to my nose. I think: about my husband, I touch: my body, I go to sleep.

*

So big, so deep. This house. Passages, doors, staircases. Once I got lost, went into a room that was out of bounds, I think, there was a desk and a wardrobe, and in the wardrobe there was a shoebox. And in the box some ancient photos and some glass slides showing a little girl with a hoop, a lady with a parasol, a moustachioed gentleman and views of a large town – buildings, streets, trams and the banks of a river. There was also a double photo, the same image twice over in a rectangular mount. Very odd. A retouched photo of some description, something like an engraving of a rose, in black and white, heightened here and there by a splash of red paint. And underneath was written

FLOWER OF DEATH

There was also an old stereoscope in the wardrobe. I slid the image in and looked at it. Now there was only one flower, but deep as a well, thrown into relief and bright like an eye staring at me.

My wedding day, I remember, was stormy. At five in the afternoon, as we climbed into the cars, we were dazzled by the exceptionally bright light. I squinted at the sky through the car window. It was dark grey, like a sheet of steel. I craned my neck trying to see where this blinding light was coming from, but there was no gap in the dark layer of cloud. Everything was frozen in this gloom and light. We left the village and picked up speed. Entirely surrounded by trees; giant, foaming, pieces of brain spat out of the apple green sky, glistening, hurled against the windscreen, against the windows.

Through the window I watch the birds running about in the grass, little moving spots of black, they are blackbirds, with yellow beaks, it's exciting in all this brilliant green, long round bodies which come and go greedy in the sunlight, flutter in your hand, at the back of the legs, at the back, of the throat, I melt, into my curtains, my white dress, put them in my dress, my loves, the grass smells, the grass smells strongly, she, speaks, to me, she, lays, me down, down softly.

At night, the sound of a cricket. I go down to the kitchen, I have a drink of milk, I sleep with my head in my arms, my arms on the table, and I dream, like a white whale I dream in the deep sea.

When I think about him. My eardrums pound, I feel like vomiting, passing out. I bang my head against the walls which separate me from my love.

I spent all day pacing round the room. I looked out of the window. The park, isolated, separated from the street by railings as high as they are rusty. The gardener is often there mowing the lawn around the house. Parts of the garden have been dug over. In the turned over soil he plants flowers, prunes trees, potters around the least bit of vegetation as if it were some woman he never tires of caressing with his large hands.

But nearer the railings it is all overgrown. Brambles, spiders. Marthe and René (the gardener) live in the old stables.

I'm happy just to watch through the window. I'm waiting for my lover. Sometimes I see something move, an insect, a blackbird, a dark flash, and I think it's him. Or else I imagine that he is hidden behind the curtain of willows.

The plane is still climbing, just a shiny dot

with a long white vapour trail. The blue of the sky starts to sparkle, I see a woman looking through the porthole. A mass of long curly blond hair, fastened in a black hairband. Her eyes staring at me. L. The plane disappears and carries her away, to the other side of the sky.

The plane drops into a thick bank of cloud, hiccups in pockets of air. Stringy grey shreds grab at the porthole.

DON'T WALK. The letters emerge almost imperceptibly from the mist. Odd place for a sign like that, she thinks, as she looks at the wing, its flaps lifting slowly, gaping in silence, blind and heavy, marking time for the descent. There is the sound of the undercarriage being lowered. The plane comes out under the fleecy mass and the first houses appear through the rain-lashed window.

'Here we go again, it'll rain like this until next summer. That's all there is in Bordeaux. Rain and wine. Are you staying long?'

'Three days. While I sort out some business.'

The taxi passes in front of a dark cathedral, turns into a gloomy passageway with a glimmer of the river visible at the other end. It plunges into a labyrinth of paved alleyways, comes out on a pedestrian street, clears a path through the dark raincoats and pulls up in front of the newly cleaned stone façade of a hotel.

L hasn't been back to the city since school-days, since her escape . . . Adolescence, memories in black and white, the occasional flash of red . . .

She has three hours before the funeral. The windows of the room look out on the street. The rain has stopped. Pigeons perch on ledges, strut on the damp pavements. L goes downstairs.

The air shimmers in the silky light after the rain. On a fruit stall a cardboard sign propped up against bottles without labels full of a white-ish brew says: VIN NOUVEAU.

L carries on further, towards the place de la Bourse and the river. She waits for a gap in the heavy traffic, and finally manages to get across the six noisy lanes of the quayside. When she finally reaches the heavy, yellow water of the Garonne she remembers what the taxi driver had told her about 'the Stream': the recent floods, a huge wave suddenly breaking over the slip-road, inundating the flow of cars driving into town.

The current suddenly draws itself together

and stops. Across its full width the river seems to be holding its breath. On the far side L makes out the muddy banks. Alice was probably born somewhere in those reeds. Alice, whom I tried so hard to forget, and why? Poor Alice, poor mad child. What room is there for her in this methodical structure of my life – studies, flirtations, engagement, first job, career plan . . .? The wind carries a faint, nauseous smell of salt from the estuary. The tide is coming in.

The men from the undertakers lower the coffin into the grave. L is alone. She gathers up a fistful of earth, drops it on the polished wooden box with a dull thud. When the hole has been filled in with large shovelfuls of earth, she stands a while beside the freshly turned rectangle. She never knew her uncle, and yet her heart is as heavy as a stone. The deserted cemetery exudes a heavy air; it grates against the ribs with every breath.

Only me to see you off. My last remaining family. Are you as alone in death as in life? . . . Look at the setting . . . stone, cross, grey sky, cut flowers, labyrinth, silence. I can see it coming, death. Masks for all at the joke-shop: horror, tears, promises, peace . . . it's just as deceptive as life. Those two, they'll do anything to make themselves interesting.

The wind lifts the dead leaves, nudges her in the back. When she reaches the end of the path, L turns back to look at the grave. In the fading light of an autumn afternoon she sees the silhouette of a woman, slightly sturdy but with a good figure and very elegant, dressed in a black outfit, dark hair tied in a chignon, kneeling before the grave. Only the white skin of her neck as she bends over the stone is visible.

L retraces her steps, struggling against the wind. But as she approaches the woman walks away quickly, without turning round. L tries to catch her up, she calls out. Madame! But the woman starts running down the soaking wet path, the heels of her shoes digging into the earth, the seams of her black stockings splashed with mud.

As a token of her presence, a spray of wine-coloured dahlias lies on the grave.

Rue de la Fusterie. A gloomy paved street. L grips in her hand the keys which the solicitor has just handed over. The taxi drops her at the corner of the rue Maubec.

'Surely you don't live here?'

'Wait for me.'

She pushes the heavy entrance door, which has been left open. A constant, urgent roll of African drums rises from the cellar and reverberates around the broad stone stairway. Behind the door a sheet of writing paper has been taped on to the flaky, dark blue paintwork. On it is written in red ink: DO NOT LEAVE THE DOOR OPEN.

After the third floor, access to the top storey is by a steep, narrow, wooden staircase. L has to jiggle the key in the lock before she manages to open it.

A very long corridor, with bare floorboards. The electricity has been cut off. L guides herself in the dark by holding on to the wall. At the end of the corridor another door. A square-shaped room, built in under the roof. On a pedestal table in a corner of the room, a ceramic vase, dark, almost navy blue in colour, and a wilting bouquet of red roses with black markings, soaking in its own sickly smell.

There are three other doors along the corridor, leading off into former servants' rooms. The first is a kitchen, with dark nooks and crannies. In the bathroom cabinet an open tube of toothpaste, from which a violet pulp emerges, seething like the burst vein of a bull. A small window looks out on a tiny interior courtyard, a four-storey well with an odd mixture of bric-à-brac piled up at the bottom. Lying on its back, a large plastic doll catches the light in its glassy eyes.

At each floor the cracked, grey wall is punctuated by a window. At the third, L catches sight of a slim, dark-haired man through the grubby pane. He is naked, standing motionless with his back to her in front of a luminous shape which seems to be a full-length mirror. Taken by surprise, L jerks her head away. A moment later, she looks again to check what she saw, but there is no one there.

There are two more attic rooms leading off the corridor. The rhythm of the African drums from the cellar is getting faster, as if the players are beating a frenetic path towards some goal which gets ever nearer, only to elude them again. In each room a skylight lets in a glimmer of sky. On the roof opposite a tabby cat freezes and stares straight at her.

The first room, next door to the kitchen, seems to be Charles's room. There is a pile of clothes in the wardrobe; hanging up, a raincoat, a few dark suits, a couple of dozen ties.

In the second room, an identical wardrobe contains a rather stranger treasure. It is empty except for the long shelf at the top, which is stocked with a whole range of jamjars (with shreds of partially removed labels still hanging on them), and wine and champagne bottles. Each of these glass containers, both clear and coloured, contains delicately crumpled piles of women's stockings.

I was still in bed, Marthe had just brought me my breakfast and opened the shutters and windows to the sun already high in the sky, I was sucking my finger dripping with rose petal jam, when he leaped into the frame. A cat. Ginger, striped, green eyes, well you know, cat's eyes. He looked at me, motionless, then he opened his mouth and miaowed. Or whatever cats do. Perhaps, in his defiant way, what he was really saying was 'Alice!' I didn't say anything. He leaped to the ground and came towards me, gliding on his little padded paws, his tail erect and quivering only at the tip.

With a hop he was up on the lace bedspread. A miaow, a purr, friends already. Up to me to respond. My hand on his collar, soft stroke down his spine, ready to climb to the base of the tail, will he let me? Then we're off again, more languid this time, tickling behind the ears, on the neck, ruffling the fur, then the toboggan ride to the end of the tail, which goes from exclamation mark to question mark, swinging lasciviously and tickling my cheek. Ah, what lovely manners! Pussies are supposed to like milk, but this one doesn't object to my coffee; he dips his nose in, laps it up, licks his chops, three leaps and he's off. Framed in the window, a flame leaping into the sun, then nothing. A strange sort of bird, that cat!

My lover has two long dimples when he laughs, white teeth and a glint in the eye. Everything becomes joyful, tender and violent when he arrives. I have long baths so that my flesh is more soft and fragrant. For him I want to be dark, damp and luminous like the garden: beautiful enough to die for.

The cat came back with a blue and yellow bird in its teeth, a blue tit, I think. He leaped to the floor with his prey, looking into my eyes. Or was it I who . . .? He dropped it, the little thing was still alive, blue and yellow, it started jerking about with its broken wings, crying out, and when it crossed the room, and with claws and teeth I'm coming after you, what fun, what fun, I go through the window, the grass, outside, I jump, I run through the grass, I hang from the weeping willow with both hands, I stay there, I wait.

Then I am stretched out on the ground, I slide off my sandals, I roll in the fresh green, on one cheek, on the other, it tickles the soles of my feet, the leaves flow down to conceal me, I close my eyes, my body rocking I fall asleep, I fall asleep, and I don't fall asleep, I see the scene again, the first, I sway and I see, water, the belly, I am in the swaying belly, curled up with myself, the other who I am, the other who is me, and yet I am outside, I see my mother and the swollen water of the river, she is crouching in the grass at the river's edge, our mother is gasping for breath, ready to deliver me into the world, to separate me from myself. Pearls of sweat glisten on her forehead. She holds her huge belly with both hands, catches her breath, moans again, from weariness or relief. Fat raindrops strike the yellow surface of the river, forming concentric circles which slowly expand and overlap. Under the long, tight lines of rain the surface of the water becomes a carpet of thorns.

Again she gasps for breath. She has been told that to lessen the pain you must breathe quickly, she does her best but the pain remains, remains unbearable. She stops herself from crying out, only the sweat again streaming from her pale forehead. Half upright, she takes a couple more steps towards the water, near where the branches of the tree sheltering her are lower. Her dress is drenched by the rain, her hair is dripping down her cheeks. She hangs on, her hand wrapped round a branch. She is alone. The contractions are coming faster. A warm liquid gushes down the inside of her thighs. Now she feels a weight pushing downwards. She pushes as well, pushes with all her strength, stops for a minute then tries again, her face screwed up with the effort.

She doesn't know how long she has been there, everything is fading already. Suddenly a baby emerges, and straight afterwards another. When these red creatures cry out she picks them up. It has stopped raining. Her feet make a sucking noise when she pulls them out of the mud.

She reaches out a hand to the large bag left lying in the wet grass and takes out a pair of scissors and a towel. She cuts the umbilical cord of the two swarthy girls, takes them to the river and washes them. Then she opens her dress, takes out her swollen breasts and feeds her two children.

She now feels attached to her babies like an animal. Her original idea had been to put the newborn into a boat and set it adrift. She had visited this spot many times before and there had always been a fisherman's boat moored at the landing-stage.

But the boat isn't there. The young woman is exhausted, she is bleeding. She wraps the babies in the towel, holds them next to her and goes to sleep. It is dark when she wakes up. The twins are crying, she offers them her breasts. Their four hands are like birds' feet, their hair is very dark and their cheeks transparent like moonflesh. She goes to lay them under the landing-stage, well wrapped in the towel, at the spot where the boat normally is. She feels nothing now. Perhaps she has become a ghost, or merely a slice of flesh flayed alive by blades of steel. She leaves without looking back.

The next day, at dawn, a fisherman discovers the two babies in their white bed. One of us is wailing with all its might. The other is dead.

*

When I woke up, the willow above my head was shaking its branches with the sound of crumpled tissue paper. With elephantine slowness, the long brushes swung towards my bedroom, whose open window was like a yellow hole.

I looked behind me. The other three willows. Also signalling me to go back.

I thought I saw a shadow flit among the bushes down at the end of the garden. I got up and walked slowly around the house towards the main gate.

I had to go to the end of the path, unrolled in front of me like a red carpet. I went the whole way moving from tree to tree, like a thief, stopping behind each tree trunk to get my breath back, in spite of the infinite slowness of my movements. The gravel rasped under my sole: 'Help!' 'Watch out!' Finally I reached the gate. Locked, but it was the same at boarding school. At the side there is a spot where the bars are more widely spaced. I squeezed myself up inside and passed through.

I read the plaque which was fixed next to the bell. 'Doctor Blanche's Rest Home.' Funny name. I will tell Doctor Blanche he should change it to 'love home'. Since my husband brought me here I have worn myself out deliciously, endlessly dying of happiness and love.

I ventured out into the street, but there was nothing and nobody there. I walked as far as the crossroads along the high railings which were choked by the jumble of brambles and bushes pressed up against the outer walls.

At the rounded corner of the pavement I stopped. Balancing first on one foot then the other, I looked right and left down the street. In fact, it was little more than a chalky strip of road, full of potholes, ramps and other bumps.

I ran back the way I had come. The road leaped, the railings leaped. I squeezed back through the gate, ran back under the willows, hoisted myself in through the window, pulled the shutters to, closed everything, the dead blue tit in the middle of the room was lost in the darkness, I undressed, I climbed into bed, my ocean of a bed, my head under the covers and in the blackness I touched everything, smelled everything, recognised everything.

I know he doesn't want me to go out. The outside is bad for me. I didn't tell him that she came back in a dream and called me. The one called Lucile, whom I call L.

I stayed all day by the window, but neither my love nor the cat came. Yet I had placed a saucer of milk on the sill and slipped my wedding dress on and off several times. By the end of the day the milk had separated: a congealed island of white curd floating in a pool of whey. I gathered the cheese with my fingers and ate it.

A light, dirty rain dampens the walls. A line of cars waits patiently in the rue Saint-James, stuck behind a lorry, before reversing awkwardly into the even narrower rue de Guienne.

Stockings in bottles. L also found, inside the school desk, five small spiral-bound notebooks, filled with cramped writing listing names of streets and names of women. Charles was sixty-seven when he died. Splashes of yellow mud around the seam of the black stockings. I must have a fever. Instead of heading off to catch her plane, L sends the taxi away, goes back to the hotel and books in for another night.

In the morning, the sky is blue, freshly cleaned. Open all the windows, get rid of the smell of death, get the electricity meter working again. L pours the stinking water from the wilting roses down the sink and arranges them in their vase on the pedestal table, which she places in the centre of the drawing room.

Then she installs herself in the second bedroom, the one with the stockings in bottles and the notebooks, empties her case, finds some white sheets in the other wardrobe with which she makes the bed.

I know you can't see or hear me, Uncle Charles. But I have discovered that I owe this to you. To stay a while. Sleep next to you, at least next to the room where you slept. I have always been so sensible. A little foolishness for an old fool, in short. Those stockings are like something you might have wanted to say to me. Something like: 'Stay a while longer. You're at home here. Live at home, long enough to welcome the guest you are expecting.' But which guest?

Sugary melodies rise up from the first floor. 'To all the girls . . .' A whole Julio Iglesias LP. When she arrived that morning, L noticed the neighbour, a fat, middle-aged Spanish woman in a black dress, busy watering the geraniums on her landing with a miniature watering can. The sort of woman who knows all there is to know about the people in the building. L goes downstairs.

The stairwell is filled by the heavy aroma of meat stew. On a label next to the bell, in elongated letters carefully traced in blue ink, is the name: Remedios Fernandez. Madame Fernandez opens her door wide, letting out hostile waves of cooking smells and the cloying sounds of the record being played on dud equipment. She guards the door to her lair, leaving the young woman standing on the doormat. From there L can see a room very much like her uncle's kitchen, gloomy and furnished in an old-fashioned way, with a table covered with a flower-patterned oilcloth and surrounded by formica chairs, and a dresser piled high with objects, dishes, postcards, baby photos, various knick-knacks ('Souvenir of . . .'), a plastic bull and a bottle of holy water from Lourdes.

L introduces herself politely, explains that she would like a little chat about her deceased uncle. Remedios looks down at her, her dark eyes hemmed with a rich fringe of black lashes, fixed on her in a quiet, steady gaze.

Madame Fernandez doesn't immediately reply. L feels as if her words have been swallowed up by the violins and the white-teethed voice of the crooner, carried off by the dulling power of the enticing, spicy smell of the stew (something heavy and red-blooded) simmering away, braising for hours, in a cast-iron pan at the back of the cooker.

L stares at the gossamer hairnet holding Remedios's salt and pepper chignon in place, with the aid of numerous hairpins, and begins to repeat her question. But the moment she opens her mouth her neighbour turns round (L notices the broad tortoise-shell comb placed between her neck and her chignon), rushes over to the left hand corner of the room, to the narrow, high shelf unit containing magazines, records, the record player and the television. The music has just stopped. Remedios lifts the pick-up arm, leaving the needle riding in the air above the last grooves of the record. Then she comes back to L.

'You are Monsieur Delassalle's niece?'

'Yes.'

'To be honest, I didn't know Monsieur Delassalle that well. I've only lived here for twenty years.'

'Twenty years . . . He bought the apartment eight years ago . . .'

'Yes, but he lived there for thirty years, at least. Didn't you know?'

'I didn't know my uncle at all.'

'Oh, he was a good man. Never made a noise, never had people round . . . Not like that lot upstairs . . .'

'He must have had someone to do his housework?'

'He did. Me. Every Thursday morning. He was very tidy, I soon got it done. Once a year my daughter helped me with the spring cleaning.'

'And . . . he never spoke to you?'

'No. Once he showed me a photo of the time he was a singer at the Grand Theatre. That's all.'

'He was a singer at the Grand Theatre?'

'Didn't you find the photo? Dressed in a shiny suit . . . Oh, a fine figure of a man!'

'I knew he worked for the Council . . .'

'That was in his later years. Before that he was a policeman as well.'

'And when you moved in?'

'He was already working at the town hall. He left every morning at twenty to nine and came home around twenty past six. Sometimes he went out again, or came home a bit later.'

'And when he retired?'

'He still left in the morning and came home in the evening. More or less the same.'

'And all these years he never had anyone round?'

'Never.'

'Never . . . any women?'

'Never. Not that he couldn't have had, if he'd wanted. I mean . . . a man on his own, one so distinguished . . . I wouldn't have minded . . .'

Back in her flat, with Iglesias's banal refrains knocking holes in the floor again, L thinks about the photo of Charles in his opera singer's garb. And about Madame Fernandez's question: Didn't you find it? No, I didn't find it. Nor any documents offering insight into his former life – apart from the notebooks and the jars of stockings (insofar as you could call those documents, and derive any conclusive evidence from them). Not even a photo of his wife, Liliane, who died young, and of whom you would have expected him to keep some special souvenir. L is troubled by the thought that this strange man was her uncle.

She takes the five small notebooks out of the desk in her room. She spreads out her map of the town on the floor beneath the attic window, and looks for the streets whose names are listed in one of the books.

The lists of names apparently mark out various itineraries, at the end of which Charles has almost always written a number (the number of a building?), sometimes a woman's first name, sometimes a dash or question mark.

There must be more than two hundred itineraries in the five notebooks. None of them has a date. L follows a number of itineraries on her map. Most of them start in the town centre. Some of them reach as far as the outskirts.

Charles was killed crossing the rue du Loup, knocked down by a car. Perhaps he was following a woman ... Or perhaps he wanted to kill himself. But you don't kill yourself like that. So what sort of man was he?

'You're looking at the town plan? Oh, I'm sorry, I startled you ... Didn't you hear me knock? Excuse me ...'

Slim, very dark hair, and dark, mocking eyes. He makes to go, but then changes his mind and moves further into the room.

'I'm your downstairs neighbour. Hugues. I'm very pleased you have inherited the flat from Charles. So, you've moved into this room ... The room of love ... A good choice.'

'Did you know my uncle well? I'm not staying here very long.'

'Long ... I love that word. Look, since we're going to be neighbours, why don't you come round for a drink at my place. What do you say?'

His place is a real artist's garret, jam-packed with junk. Dust dances in a ray of sunlight. He makes some space on his make-shift table – a large chipboard panel resting on trestles, covered with canvases and drawing paper, boxes bristling with pencils, rolled-up or split tubes and pots of paint, brushes in all sizes, sticks of ink and penholders, black cases of twisted steel instruments like miniature surgical implements, and a fat, convex magnifying glass like a triple-thick spectacle lens.

Turning round, Hugues catches the young woman gazing at his shoulders and he smiles. He brings over two wineglasses and an already opened bottle of wine. He displays the label before pouring.

'You're a painter?'

On the wall, paintings in cold colours and ink-drawings obsessively portray a violent, ghostly world, where roughly outlined, superimposed human figures – whose expressions are nevertheless quite clear – fuse into the background and into each other. On a pedestal table, a chess board, the pieces perfectly aligned with the exception of one black pawn and one white pawn, each advanced by two squares.

'I've already met my first-floor neighbour.'

'The only person in the building who gets up before midday.'

'You work at night?'

'I paint, or I study human characters to improve my painting . . . It comes to the same thing. Would you like to sit for me this evening?'

At the end of the room, leaning diagonally in the corner, L thinks she sees the long mirror which she spotted the previous day from her uncle's apartment when the figure of a naked man appeared momentarily before it. He refills the glasses and turns his own round slowly in the light.

'Did you know Charles well?'

His skin-tight, almost threadbare black wool jumper shows off his long, slender muscles. Maybe three or four years older than me, not more than thirty. She empties her glass.

Slowly, heavily, the wine spins its sad dance in her body. L walks up the hallway without the light on, bumping against the walls, she crosses the kitchen, pushes open the bathroom door, bends over the toilet, sticks two fingers down her throat and vomits.

She takes her clothes off, gets into bed and wraps herself in the coarse sheets. She closes her eyes. I am a speck, a sparkling speck of dust, everything spins around me, drags me into its cosmic movement, nothing to hang on to, nothing to recognise myself by. I and me, strange words, they go aboard a boat, which one propels the other? She throws a leg out of the bed, touches the floor with the tips of her toes. Through her eyelids passing clouds sweep the room with large, light shadows.

Her watch lies on the bedside table like a spider or a bird in flight, the two round branches of the leather strap on each side of the face like wings or the legs of an enormous trapdoor spider. With her bad dreams still weighing heavily on her chest, she struggles to emerge from sleep, staring at the object in her half-awake state with a vague sense of dread.

The rue Maubec leads down to the quayside. Although the dark, heavy mass of water is opaque in the evening shadow, L can sense the powerful currents at work within the river. The flickering fireflies thrown on its surface by the lamps on the Pont-de-Pierre cannot dissipate the dull, troubling call, from a mute mouth, which cuts through the town in a cajoling curve, with a melancholy elegance.

L walks along the quayside till she reaches the first shed, a huge, gloomy disused depot, on the front of which, in spaced-out letters on a faded royal blue background, is the inscription: COMPAGNIE TRANSATLANTIQUE. She crosses, goes round the north side of the place de la Bourse and heads back towards the centre along the rue du Pont-de-la-Mosque.

Here and there, the pavement exudes a strong smell of urine. A drunk appears out of nowhere, staggers towards her vomiting sweet nothings. The street is deserted, apart from a line of prostitutes, each standing stationary in her doorway, flashing a thigh. Black stockings, fish-net stockings, white flesh spilling over suspenders, the only real, pale light in the street.

L makes her way home through the back-streets, stepping up her pace a bit. At the corner of the rue de la Fusterie she stops at a grocer's and picks out some fruit. The Arab who serves her is a prince. He smiles and calls her 'gazelle'. He picks up the figs with great care and places them delicately in the paper bag. His dark eyes envelop her in velvet. She would gladly go away with him, to his country, she imagines a long room, rugs, a blue and white wall, blue in the half near the ceiling, she imagines that dividing line half-way up the wall, where have I seen that? That dividing line, so luminous, so serene . . . Outside, the earth is red, the sun beats down. L lives with the women in the shade of the house, time stands still, L feels good, L and the other women await the night, the man . . .

L pays and goes, L is a young, free woman, the Arab has never drunk his steaming tea in the room with the blue and white walls, he also likes modern women. And L is horrified at the thought of being shut away, horrified.

The door of the building has been left open onto the gaping dark stairwell. My neighbour said he would do my portrait.

He makes some mulled wine, with cinnamon and sugar. Normally draw nudes, he says. Perhaps you should give it a miss. Why me? After all, two strangers. L undresses. He prepares his materials, doesn't look at her. He seems to find this quite normal.

He fastens a large sheet of paper to a plywood

board hanging on the wall and pours some water into a little iron dish with a sloping base. He is still wearing his black jumper next to his skin, he bends forward, he concentrates, he is absorbed. This gives his face a look of innocence, something almost child-like, why are men so beautiful? He picks out a stick of ink, rubs it gently against the basin. Gripping her blouse to her breast with one hand, the naked L watches with a shudder as the particles of ink float and become diluted in the water, which gradually blackens until it becomes shiny and opaque.

Hugues spreads a sheet over an old armchair and makes her sit, with her head tilted over the back, her long blond hair hanging down, her legs stretched over the armrest. With sure, precise, almost brusque movements, as if everything had been planned. Now he gathers together the brushes on the perfectly arranged table, places them under the lamp, examines them, blows on them, wets the tips with his tongue. They haven't spoken since he started his preparations, and it feels as if this silence is making her more naked, not in an indecent way.

'It'll be nicer like this . . .'

His voice is soft, soft and warm. Hugues parts the legs of his model a little and pours some wine down the inside of her thighs. The wine makes dark red streaks on her skin, then flows onto the white sheet, where it makes a more vivid stain.

'Woman's blood . . .'

'But you're using black ink . . . There is no colour . . .'

'I'll find some colour. Just for that part. The inside of the thighs . . . I have to try . . .'

Hugues seems to be holding his breath, as if concentrating his whole self in his left hand, then he goes to work.

He dashes off a couple of lines on the paper, pauses, then starts again. She doesn't watch, she simply concentrates on not moving, which soon causes her to ache. She can feel the cold on her skin, but there is a warmth building up inside her taut body, increasingly so now that Hugues accompanies his work with a monologue perhaps destined for himself alone.

'You want me to tell you about your uncle? You are beautiful, with your red thighs . . . Your uncle, my friend Charles, had unusual tastes, you know. You found the notebooks and the stockings in the wardrobe? Charles . . . He loved women. But not just any old women. Women who loved love . . . Women who wore . . . stockings . . . He followed them in the street . . . And he kept . . . their stockings . . . black stockings, seamed stockings, silk stockings, such sheer stockings . . . Not whores' stockings, women's stockings, real women . . . real . . . sluts – pardon me . . . It's the word Charles used . . . But he said it with respect and love . . . these women are so devoted to making men dream . . . with their tight, split skirts . . . they climb on the bus and the cloth stretches taut on their bums, rides up . . . you can see the tops of their stockings, the darker stripe . . . the end of a suspender . . . bare flesh . . . That's what Charles liked . . . Charles, the little anonymous functionary, his life appeared so austere, so ordered . . . That was his fantasy . . . seeking out women's stockings . . . He had his own routes, codes, secrets . . . A dream of his own . . . Don't move, you're perfect . . .'

L looks at her violet-coloured thighs. If she had stayed naked in the cold until she turned blue, if she had been beaten until her veins burst, if a dark, thick, odorous blood were flowing from her sex. If in an Italian ditch, one morning . . .

'Me,' Hugues continued, 'I'm not like Charles. The women I dream about are not those who make you dream, who provoke fantasy. They are the ones I make myself, the ones which my dreams create, the ones my art models and brings to life . . .'

L gets up.

Washes her legs.

Gets dressed slowly, more and more painfully.

She will have to leave. Hugues still obstinately a stranger. An enemy lurking in the shadow, repudiating her, fascinating her. Whom I detest. She is in the diagonal shadow of the open door, ready to leave, to tear herself away from him, when the words come out of her mouth, she asks. Sleep with you.

He smiles imperceptibly, his eyes turn away, he bends over the table and says it is too early for him, he wants to do some more work. If only he would kiss me, show one sign of tenderness. She waits for a while, she feels so uncomfortable. But nothing happens, he lets her leave without making any gesture, with only a slightly sorry smile, a polite smile. She doesn't close the door, she disappears into the dark hole of the stairwell.

A little later, in bed, she hears Hugues' door open and shut and his footsteps descending the stairs. She lies motionless in the dark, her eyes wide open.

L and I waited for the night to come. The dormitory doors were closed, but the fanlights in the showers were easy to open. The night before, once the lights went out and everyone, including the monitor, was asleep, we returned to the showers. We climbed up to the fanlights, sat on the tiled sill, and stayed there watching the sky until morning.

It's strange watching the sky all night, you see how much it fluctuates. The stars all move slowly, all together, like some massive caravan . . . Then there are the shooting stars, aeroplane lights, satellites, all in a great noisy silence . . . There's no time to get bored. When day comes you think: 'over already!' It's like when they turn up the lights after a concert you've really liked. But at the same time it's the best bit. Dawn's really weird. There's no one moment when you can say: 'that's it, there's the dawn!'. You've just got time to say: 'there's the start of the dawn' when the night ends its flight. Then: 'there's the end of the dawn, it was a beautiful dawn'. Then it's already morning.

I'm the one who called her L. She was like an angel. To my mind L was 'Aile' – 'wing' – and also 'Elle' – 'she'. Above all, it was the secrecy of it. Just an initial, that means that there is something concealed. Everyone else used her daylight name, I alone gave her a little darkness. L used to say that she wished that she didn't have any parents, like me. One night, when we were in the showers, she stretched out on the tiles and tried an experiment. I was kneeling beside her and I had to hold out my hand to give her my energy and make sure I didn't move. She concentrated long and hard. I was afraid she might catch cold, lying there quite rigid in her nightdress on the floor. I don't know what possessed me, I was cold as well, I lay down on top of her.

She showed no reaction, her eyes remained shut, as if she were oblivious to everything. Her body grew warmer and warmer, mine too, waves passed between us, ever more intense, I no longer knew where the division was between my breasts and hers, my stomach and hers. I placed my lips on hers, put my hands in hers, to make the fusion even more perfect. She was breathing more quickly, I followed, breathing in the air which had just emerged burning from her veins.

She still didn't move. But she began to tremble, like me, from head to toe, our mouths opened, our tongues met, then it was as though we lost consciousness, or rather the opposite, the waves became more and more violent, until finally birds flew out of our mouths, birds of night or of paradise, singing their raucous, gentle songs.

When we got up, she told me that she had managed to get out of her body. Her spirit had risen up above us and she had seen us both, her lying on the ground and me sitting by her side holding her hand and then she had gone far away, she had travelled through time, to the moment of her birth where it had been revealed to her that she was the reincarnation of my twin sister. 'You and I, we are the same spirit in two different bodies,' she said. Her eyes were shining.

I didn't believe it. My twin sister doesn't have a name, she can't have a body. And besides, L is much more beautiful than me, and blond. I didn't say anything, she was just being nice.

They put my sister's little body in a white sheet and in the end it disappeared as if it had never existed. Life selected me, but I am the twin of Death.

After we went over the wall it took us two nights to hitch down to Italy. We were there a long time, staying with the nuns. They had found us in a ditch on the second morning. We had broken bones, bruises all over and blood on the inside of our thighs, but we didn't care, it didn't even hurt. We were simply holding on to each other, refusing to be separated. One of them spoke French, and asked us what had happened, but we couldn't remember anything and besides we didn't want to talk. We didn't say a thing for weeks.

We were happy in that convent. It was high up on a cliff, with nothing else around it. We got up early and went to bed early, the sisters left us to our own devices. During this time we got used to not opening our mouths, except to eat, but we ate hardly anything, especially me. Right at the edge of the cliff there was a sort of small stone terrace and we sat there on the ground with our backs to the wall all day long.

When the sun came out it seemed to caress us, we didn't move an inch and we felt good, it warmed us like the stone, as if we were stone ourselves . . . And when the clouds passed over we became cold and grey, we curled up our arms and legs and waited for the wind to clear the clouds and bring back the sun. We were fine there. Everything was peaceful, it was as if time had stopped. We would have liked to stay there forever.

Then the men in uniform came to fetch us and put us on the plane. They took us to the hospital. After three days, L left and I was kept in.

Later, she came to see me. When she came into my room she turned pale. It was as if she didn't recognise me. It was as if she no longer thought at all that she was the reincarnation of my twin sister, as if I even scared her. She even seemed to find it impossible to say my name. Not surprising – I looked like a corpse. I hardly said anything to her, so she had an excuse to leave straight away. She didn't ask what had happened to me, how I was feeling, nothing. Tiny beads of sweat appeared on her face, she said she would come again, she smiled at me as if everything were normal, then she left. I went back to my room, I was well rid of her. After that, no one came to see me.

Everyone encouraged me to get some sun, but I wouldn't budge, I stayed indoors, and that's how I got through it. Besides, I wasn't ill, I'd just had enough of people. They obviously didn't grasp that, but I couldn't care less. Alone in bed I felt just fine. I slept whenever, day or night. When I woke up I remembered my dreams and wrote them down. Once I had done that I was happy, I didn't feel like vomiting any more. Thus I became like I was before.

You should put it all behind you. That's what he says, my lover. Now that I'm happy with him. This morning I found traces of blood on my sheet, dark blood like wine. At first I was afraid. It had been several years since I last had my period. Marthe took the sheet away, I told her it was the blood of my lost virginity. You should have seen her face. I laughed and laughed . . .

A whole week waiting for something to happen. L is like a woman on a blind date in a bar. The woman waits. Perhaps he has been held up. Or maybe he is already there and they haven't recognised each other. The sign they had agreed on wasn't clear enough. Just a newspaper, but several men in the bar have the same newspaper. The woman tries to size them up discreetly, without looking desperate. She starts thinking that perhaps she doesn't make the grade, that the man has already spotted her but decided that she wasn't what he was looking for. But it's just a passing doubt. Deep down she knows the meeting will take place.

Five more minutes, then I'll leave. But the five minutes pass and she extends her deadline, because she can't stand the thought of not seeing it through to the end.

An old town house on the cours du Chapeau-Rouge. On the second floor, a large drawing-room, made dark by thick wall-hangings, serves as a waiting room. But I have to get home. Pack your case, take the plane, go. Get up, don't just sit there.

Everywhere doors, deserted corridors. The man in the white coat leads her to his surgery, which is as dark as the waiting-room. He sits behind his desk and asks the usual idiotic question doctors ask: How are you feeling? As if you could answer anything else. Bad.

A hunting dog snoozes under the table. The room is stuffy, all the instruments are old and of dubious cleanliness. L maintains that she still feels really unwell.

He asks her to remove her blouse, sounds her lungs, her throat, and declares everything to be fine. He lights a cigarette, sits down behind his desk again and keeps the fag-end in the corner of his mouth until the end of the consultation.

The dog under the table twitches and starts moaning; he is dreaming, his head resting between his paws. L insists that she is really very unwell. She even tells him that she has nightmares, that she has trouble sleeping. Finally he gives her a sick note. This is the first time that she has resorted to such deception, normally she hates it, and the tacit complicity which it involves. She leaves quickly, without looking round.

Sometimes she wants to believe that she is staying there because of Hugues. Yet Hugues repels her as much as he attracts her. She hasn't been back to his place since the posing session. She passed him one day on the stairs. He reminded her that he hadn't finished the drawing, and she should come round again. He was on his way to his apartment with Véronique, Madame Fernandez's daughter, who also lives on the first floor, next door to her mother. No, it is out of the question that I should be there for him again.

Nevertheless, she feels ready for a meeting.

In the afternoons the building belongs body and soul to Africa. A huge, crazy heart beats in the cellar. Its dull thuds rise up the stairwell and spread out into the rooms of the apartments. Calloused hands beat painfully on taut skins, to the rhythm of the body's pulse, the pulse of the world. L holds her breath.

The neighbour on her landing, Mamadou, a charming Guinean, always greets her on the stairs in the same way:

'Hello, neighbour, how are you?'

'Fine, and you?'

'Oh, music is tough, neighbour . . .'

He shares an apartment with one of his musicians, Manu, the only white in the group. In fact, Mamadou sleeps elsewhere half the time, with one or other of his women. Mamadou has his own court. Everyone who works or hangs out with him regards him as the master. He gets invited abroad, he takes along three, four maybe five musicians, occasionally some dancers as well. But in the end he wastes his opportunities, lives from night to night, and ends up every time back in Bordeaux, partying and smoking grass with his crowd until morning.

L goes to Mamadou's place one evening. There are already people there. Aïcha, Mamadama. A white student taking notes. Manu. Some other musicians. A boy who drives across the desert every couple of months in a Peugeot and flies back having sold the car and bought some instruments and skins. And Hugues, later.

On the low table there is a large dish of *foniou*, an African cereal accompanied by a fish sauce. Martinos explains where the fish comes from, what an ugly head it has, what its nick-name is. Everyone helps themselves and tucks in hungrily. There is something sticky in the sauce. L feels like vomiting with each mouthful.

Manu talks about Véronique. Apparently she is too beautiful. 'It's a real problem for her,' he says. He suggested the solution would be to shave her head.

Véronique hasn't quite decided. She rather unwisely discussed the idea with her mother, who got into a real state. She's already had it up to here with the noise of tom-toms, all the comings and goings on the stairs, the cooking smells, the entrance door which 'they' never close, despite the sign she stuck up, so the thought of this white negro wanting to shave off her little princess's beautiful dark curls drove her spare. She yelled at Manu from her window as he was leaving the building, calling him a pimp and a filthy Arab. L asks Manu:

'What did you reply?'

'Oh, I teased her a bit . . .'

'Meaning what?'

'Oh, something along the lines of: go back where you came from!'

'You call that teasing?'

Manu laughs. L talks a little longer with Martinos, who punctuates every sentence with a peal of laughter. Mamadama stands next to the fireplace, humming to herself, langorously swaying her dancer's body. Manu is discreetly courting Aïcha. Hugues is in discussion with the desert traveller, they seem to be hatching plans for some new business between Africa and Bordeaux. Sweet Aïcha and bold Mamadama laugh and move without fear of eating up the space around them, languid, elegant, regal, with confident step, bearing and gestures more beautiful, more nonchalant, more fierce than ballet movements, as if the world belonged to them.

As L is leaving Manu reminds her:

'The hair, think about it . . . It could do you some good as well.'

At night L tosses and turns in bed, searching for sleep. With her eyes closed, she tries to think about her fiancé, but it is the image of Hugues which she keeps seeing behind her eyelids.

One time, she dreams she is making love with Mamadou. She is waiting in an antechamber, with dozens of other girls. Like all the others, she has a ticket in her hand showing her number in the queue. When she is admitted L is amazed at the sight before her: Mamadou is sitting in the lotus position, like a god in his temple, naked and motionless, his giant sex erect, resplendent. She understands that she is supposed to impale herself on it, before making way for the next in line. L starts to move up and down vigorously on his hard member, but then suddenly realises that it is not Mamadou she has straddled but Hugues, and with an unbearable pain in her heart she knows that she is merely one number among the countless many passing in procession to his body. Then she begins to cry bitterly with a disappointment and pain so acute that she wakes up.

Another night, her limbs gnawed by solitude, a solitude without escape, L thinks that perhaps, as a last resort, an orgasm might help her to find peace and sleep. She spreads her legs and begins to caress herself, half-heartedly. Nothing. She raises her pelvis further, accelerates the movement of her hands, tries to think about Hugues and summon up some erotic fantasy. Her body refuses to respond. Normally it is simple and quick. An opaque cloud of distress closes around her. She gets up, finds her way to the kitchen in the dark, opens the drawer of the dresser. In the shadow a packet of white candles. She takes one and returns to bed. Back to work, legs apart, showing herself no mercy, thinking about nothing at all now. Finally she feels a slight sensation of pleasure. It has taken so long and required such effort. She tries to make it last, to prevent it ending straight away. But she hangs on too long, it becomes diluted and finally ends in a meager climax. She lies on her back, more awake than ever, her sex sore at having been so abused by her wretched anger.

The day after the session, L wanted to have it out with Hugues. I'm here to sort out the sale of the apartment, I will tidy up a bit, empty the wardrobes of all the old junk they contain. Then quickly leave town, return home. Let him know gently that it was all over. That it had been, so to speak, a momentary aberration due to fatigue, having too much time on her hands and being a long way away from her family. Leave with a frank smile, without equivocation.

The rain envelops her room again with its

dull murmur. L selects clothes from the wardrobe, under the grim gaze of the coffins of stockings. Closing the doors, she thinks she sees in the mirror shades of purple still drawn on the palest part of her thighs, deeply ingrained, as if they had been drinking ink, as if they were gangrenous.

L goes down to Hugues' apartment. He is still in bed, asleep. His bare torso above the sheets, his dark eyelashes, his handsome face shut off. I have to tell him, nevertheless. I just wanted to say . . . It's all over. But nothing actually started. Hugues: Nothing?

She touches him on the shoulder, breathing his name in a low voice. He turns over in his sleep, an irritated look on his face, almost spiteful. His back to her.

There are large boxes of drawings stacked against the wall. L opens them and find dozens of ink drawings. Women in carnival dress, their faces often hidden by masks, their legs open; or women half-naked, but always squeezed into sophisticated underwear, which helps give them an expression at once cruel, sexual and morbid. Contrary to what Hugues claimed, none of them had posed nude as L did.

She closes the boxes and leaves, with one last

look at the sleeping Hugues, at the short black hairs on his neck delineating his ears.

L walks along the rue Sainte-Catherine, her eyes riveted on the women's legs. The crowd flows infinitely slowly over its bed of red paving-stones, reduced by the throng of umbrellas to a damp passageway enclosing this intimate humanity from which arises the smell of corpses and earth. Beneath the dresses the legs come and go. Which ones are naked at the top of the thighs, naked white thighs beyond the end of the stockings and beneath the dark mass of the sex?

L goes into the shops, buys red satin shoes, a red velvet sheath dress, crimson silk suspenders and matching knickers.

In one large store she wanders around the stocking department. Carefully chooses a pair. Steals them.

With her spoils clasped in her fingers she exits into the street. Her heart emptied by this miserable satisfaction.

She reaches the Grand Theatre, where Uncle Charles sang in his youth. The stone lightens as the sun breaks through. The negative of an intangible work of art, a figure in dialogue with space, the breeze of time, the sky, the changing, ever-renewed union of elements. Carved stone to emphasise this painful space which I also feel in the pit of my stomach and which I must feed: the void.

She walks across the flight of steps along the side of the building. She feels carried along. She goes on to the public park.

The sun warms gently, as it sometimes does on an autumn afternoon at the end of a rainy day. There is just enough breeze to cause the leaves to rustle on the trees bordering the paths. There is an exquisite smell of earth and wet grass. Two small boys play on the little island built in the middle of the waterway. Their satchels on a bench, their trousers marked by the splashes of the toboggan ride and the wooden seat of the roundabout, they run, cry, laugh. Suddenly, L has the strong sensation that Alice is walking beside her, one step behind. She would like to turn round, banish the shadow with a jerk of the head, but Alice prevents her with a hand placed firmly on her shoulder.

'Wait for me,' says Alice. She is not making any actual sound with her mouth, she is speaking without words. Merely the sense of her command resonates and radiates painfully around L.

'Wait for me,' the shadow says. 'Can't you see that you are dead? I alone can save you. You gave up, you and me. Now you've joined the game, a pawn among an endless crowd of pawns, the cohorts of everyone else. Lined up on the gigantic draughts board, moved by the finger of some old fool. But it is not enough. You have to go to the end of despair, to the limit where it turns back on itself, puts on its frightening masks of joy, appetite for life, supreme indifference, pleasure. Look at yourself, L. You aren't playing any more. You're suffocating. Are you counting on Hugues to bring you some relief by undoing the laces? I alone can rip off your bodice, cut you free of this vile scab, liberate your throbbing belly. Remember when we were young and we became one.'

She withdraws her hand and, before she disappears, adds: 'Fear is a bitch. Stroke its neck. It will follow you faithfully to the darkest corner of your room.'

There is a wind blowing in my head. I can't manage to hold on to my thoughts.

This time I left, I kept walking, I knew the town was a fair way. Eventually a car pulled up behind me, I turned round, it was black, the guy leaned over to open the door, I got in.

I left all my things at the house. Just took my bag, my white dress, my knickers, my hairbrush. And a large pair of scissors, which I stole. My feet hurt a bit, it's so long since I last wore shoes. Free, I'm free! Not a penny to my name, but I couldn't wait any longer to tell my lover. You thought I was a little girl? You'll see, I'm a grown woman now. That makes me laugh and laugh.

The guy doesn't stop talking. I don't listen to a word he says. He lets go of the steering wheel, waves his hands about, shows off, slips me the odd smile, looks at my legs.

The weather is fine, a pale sky where the car glides all alone.

He pulls over, invites me for a drink on the

terrace of a café in a square in the town centre. The mint liquid laps around the ice-cubes like the sea in a lagoon. I feel hot. He is wearing a dark suit, perfectly tailored in an expensive cloth, chic and heavy. Pointed ears, dark eyes, in his flow of words he holds my head under the water; I hold my breath and see his heavily ringed fingers slipping among the glasses with the agility of fishes with golden scales.

Don't follow him.

He gets up, I follow him, we walk up the street against the flow of the crowd, which opens to let us through, separated by our invisible swimming stroke, then empties in and out of the sluices of the department stores. In a rhythmic swell, the surge breaks over the cave of my eyes, from which salty streams overflow, a bitter juice in the corner of my lips, tears drying on my throat.

We have to walk down a corridor with tiled walls, beneath the humming neon of the hall lights. His keys, hanging from a ring in the crook of his index finger, jangle against his thigh. He opens the door with a firm, sure hand, turns the handle, shows me in and puts the bunch of keys back in his pocket.

Leather upholstery, white paper, filtered daylight, order. He puts his arm round my waist, leads me over to the sofa and sits down next to me. Touches my hair, says something. Looks at me, gets up, leaves the room.

Make a dash for the door, run down the corridor, call the lift, get back to the street, return home.

He comes back with two glasses and a bottle, pours out his fire-water which I drink in one go. He gives me a refill, smiling. Those ears! Pointed, pointed, pointed, a cat! He pours, I drink, he pours, I drink. His eyes are shining, his ears are growing, his smile is getting wider, I close my eyes, he disappears, I stretch out, I feel sleepy . . . The cat has come back, he weaves in and out under my wedding dress, I raise my petticoats to let him out from under the frills, and he comes back, head down he goes in under the tulle, his furry tail stands vertical between my knees. It's a little cat, a kitten, he fastens onto my breast, he wants to feed, he's hurting me with his teeth, I pull him away from my breast. I prepare a bottle of warm milk, the nipple is too big, I put it in my own mouth, I try sucking, the bottle swells in my hand, I'm doing my best, the bottle swells even more, then the milk starts to flow, to the back of my throat, right down between my legs where his little tongue laps it, lap my little pussy.

He comes back with some hamburgers, apple pies and coke. We could be in an American film. I ask him why his ears are pointed, he asks me if I have any ideas. He pulls a leather attaché case from under the low table, places it on his knees, opens it with his thumbs, searches among his documents, shows me some newspaper cuttings, photocopies enclosed in plastic wallets. Some of them bear his photo, the papers pass through his hands, I try to keep track, read them, but the meaning escapes me, I forget it all as I go along. Then suddenly I throw up. I try to turn my head away, but it's too late, the yellow liquid spurts out, speckled with brown and red lumps, minced meat with tomato sauce, all over the carpet, the sofa, the nice suit.

He'll be some time in the bathroom. I escape to the toilet and have a good laugh.

Mad, but has a way of making you obey him. Made me pay, that night. With his hairless body, his pointed ears and his wicked eyes, like a devil.

In the middle of the afternoon I hear a key in the lock. I dash to the entrance hall just in time to see him lock the door and slip the keys into his pocket.

He comes towards me smiling sternly. I recoil, I fall back into the chair, trapped.

He brings in the heavy glasses filled with a bitter, pissy liquid.

Tilting my head back I see a tube of metal coiling round the long stem of the lampstand like a snake.

He lets out two cries in a weird falsetto voice. Both times I crane up to see his twisted face, his upper lip drawn back over his gums. The third cry is a long drawn out death rattle, his eyelids half-closed. Then he keels over on his side.

I carefully disentangle myself and thrust my hand into the pocket of his trousers, which are now round his knees. I find the keys, a wad of notes and a well-ironed handkerchief, which I use to wipe my face and stomach. His glassy eyes seem to be looking at me. I spit on the soft mound between his legs and leave.

In the middle of the night L is woken by the sound of whispering. She can't make out the words, but she can clearly hear two voices, as if the people were in the next room. She switches on the light, gets up, does a tour of the apartment. No one there. She opens the bedroom window and looks out into the street. A car speeds past, doesn't slow down at the crossroads. Then nothing.

She can hear the conversation even more clearly from the bathroom. The sound is coming up through the pitch-black column of the interior courtyard. Down below, the doll catches the livid moonlight between its spread limbs. She still can't catch the meaning of the words, but she can tell from the whispers that the two speakers are a man and a woman. It is impossible to tell which floor they are on. She goes back to bed.

Before long the whispers turn into angry shouts. The woman in particular sounds quite worked up. Her voice is strident, high-pitched,

L doesn't catch a word of what she says. Every so often he yells back at her. Then come the long moans, interspersed with sobbing and clipped words. In spite of the tension which this invisible scene causes her, L finally falls asleep to its monotonous melody.

She wakes up late. With a headache. She goes to Hugues' place, opens the door and enters without a sound. He is still asleep. She stretches out next to him on the little bit of bed left over, lies there stiffly, barely daring to breathe. She weeps silently.

'What's wrong?' says Hugues. He doesn't seem surprised to find me there. My face must look haggard.

He makes some coffee, they drink it with a cigarette. L notices that the chess board on the pedestal table is now missing several pieces; some of those remaining, both black and white, have ventured forth into enemy territory. 'I play against myself,' Hugues replies.

L decides to tell him about the distressing conversation from last night. He listens attentively, but simply says that he didn't hear a thing. She should ask Mamadou and Manu. But L knows their voices well, and it wasn't either of them. 'Perhaps it was mine?' he says. No, she doesn't think so.

'I don't suppose it was Remedios with a lover . . . nor Véronique moaning next to her mother . . . But if you're sure you didn't dream it . . .'

L is certain she didn't, but . . . Well, yes, maybe I dreamed it.

He accompanies her to the door and suggests she spends tomorrow evening with him. What would Alice do? He wouldn't send her away like that. It must be her eyes. Eyes which eat you and swallow you up. They are all interested in her eyes. In the appetite and madness they see in them, no doubt. She must have seduced the doctors even. It isn't always deliberate, it's just the way she is. I can't say it was she who attracted the two shits who picked us up in Italy. They were killed in a car crash shortly after they left us in the ditch, I'm still happy about that. But. Alice is like a magnet. She attracts everything, including the bad.

'Make yourself pretty, we're going out and about.' He adds: 'Tomorrow evening I want you to be the best-looking.'

As he constructs a *djembé* with one of the skins and red-wood forms which the desert traveller brought back, Manu talks about the little circle which gravitates around Mamadou. So friendly. But in spite of their friendships, there are rivalries, manœuvres to win the master's favour, intrigues, resentments. How Mamadou exploits this to manipulate them all he doesn't say, but I can imagine it. 'In any case,' says Manu, 'we forget all about it in the end. After a few days we'll pat each other on the shoulder, fall into each other's arms as if nothing had happened.'

About Uncle Charles he claims to know nothing. But he talks about Hugues' former next-door neighbour, a university lecturer who had become a stone cutter for some strange reason. 'It's like that sometimes,' he says. 'Some other being within you comes to meet you . . . Ask Mamadou, he'll tell you some amazing things about that.'

'Doesn't he live here any more? The stone cutter, the lecturer . . .'

'He's dead. He was working on the Cordouan lighthouse. There was a storm blowing, no boats could get near it. By the time the helicopter arrived it was too late. His heart . . .'

'When I was a girl,' says L, 'I had a friend I thought was another me. Even though she looked nothing like me. She lived in a fantasy world, never had her feet on the ground. But it's so difficult being alone. We helped each other to live.'

L leads the conversation on to Hugues. 'Hughes is a really talented guy,' says Manu. She persists:

'Have you known him long?'

'Quite a long time, yes.'

He crouches down over the *djembé* to tighten the multicoloured strings, the sailor's twine, which stretch the skin on the instrument. There is a cracking sound each time the skin is pulled, which seems to give him pleasure.

'Look how beautiful this skin is. I can sense that it will make the *djembé* sing.'

L waits till he is finished and starts asking questions again:

'Hugues . . . Does he make a living from his painting?'

Instead of replying Manu gets up and asks her to excuse him, he has to go to a rehearsal. But as he leaves her on the doorstep he adds:

'The giant marionettes he made for the theatre . . . hasn't he told you about them?'

And again, as they go their separate ways on the stairs:

'Look after yourself . . .'

With a wink, as if to tell her that he understood.

That night an intolerable litany of complaints and cries of anger, the same distressing performance, insinuates its way into her dreams, drags her from her sleep. L gets up. Leaves her apartment silently, her arms crossed over her white nightgown. Half way down the wooden staircase she can hear the moans again, more faintly.

L descends the steps slowly, without making a sound, her ears pricked. She hasn't turned on the light. The almost full moon dispenses a yellow light through the landing window.

The moans start again and become sharper as she descends. They are like a woman's lament, almost langorous. Occasionally this lugubrious song is blotted out by the angry voice of a man. It is not Hugues' voice. It gets darker as she approaches the lower floor, but she is too afraid to turn on the light. The night envelops her, brings her over to the lament.

A faint gleam of light filters under Hugues' door. The noises are coming from his apartment. L places her hand on the latch. Breathes in. Applies pressure slowly, very slowly. The door opens.

The light from the television illuminates Hugues, stretched out on the armchair with the sheet, his legs wide open, his penis in his hand, naked. On the screen there is a woman dressed in a basque and black stockings, kneeling before a man with an erect penis, pleading with him. The man is wearing formal dress and a top hat which masks his face in shadow. The woman holds her face in her hands; it is twisted with pain, or perhaps some long and dreadful ecstasy. The man cries out, she reaches out to him, grabbing convulsively at one of the tails of his frock-coat. She seems hysterical now. Suddenly L notices that there is a third person on the screen, a woman in a carnival dress who is observing the scene from the shadows. Does she only notice her now because her eyes have become so bright? She gets up and approaches the couple, turning her princess's dress up over her stomach. Lovingly, the man takes hold of the hand of the first woman, still kneeling and hanging on to his suit, then turns to the second woman, places his penis between her red stockings and takes her standing up with violent thrusts of his pelvis.

Panting with jealous excitement, L watches Hugues' upturned face convulse.

L starts her preparation in the late afternoon with a sort of vengeful rage. She feels she will never be beautiful enough. She puts on the suspender belt, the stockings, the high-heeled shoes, the red dress, a musky perfume. She takes time over her make-up, adding colour to her pale, insomniac complexion. She has dark rings under her eyes. When the sky outside is completely black she goes down to Hugues' apartment like someone heading for a wall to bang her head against it.

The pavements glisten. L watches her every step; nevertheless she turns her ankle in her high heels. Hugues takes her into a small street and stops in the dampness of a neon light. He takes her by the shoulders, pins her back against the wall.

'It's only a game. I'll be just over there. Please, promise not to move. I'll come and get you.'

The stone is cold against her bare back. A woman walks past, her head lowered once she has glanced at her. Lucile lowers her head as well. She can barely make out Hugues standing in a doorway on the opposite side of the street. She crosses her legs, pulls down her dress so as not to show the black strip of her stockings, shivers.

A man comes, slowing down as he looks at her side-on, then carries on his way. Her nipples, tightened by the cold, stand out under the velvet. The man walks on a bit, then does an about-turn.

L remembers a wall-eyed dog, a thin hairless dog in the icy mist of a landscape in Auvergne. Abandoned village, old cemetery at the foot of the church . . . and the dog whose strange eyes blur your vision . . .

He is an immigrant, Portuguese perhaps, indeterminate age, dry body in a threadbare suit which is too big for him, chiselled face. He approaches her, grimacing with shyness.

'Excuse me, madame, how much?'

'I'm sorry?'

Another jab of pain crosses his soft face.

'How . . . how much?'

L replies in the same soft voice as his.

'You've made a mistake, monsieur. I'm waiting for someone.'

She wants to excuse herself, assure him that it doesn't matter. They have each been as stupid as the other. They might even be able to have a laugh about it. But he heads off alone into the night, his shadow elongated on the shining pavement behind him, with his hatred, his unhappiness and his shame.

This is stupid, this is stupid! L starts running, Hugues catches her up, grabs her by the shoulders, she tears herself free. In her red velvet dress L feels like a theatre curtain after the final bell. Opening up. She turns to face Hugues and speaks quietly, enunciating every word clearly, like a prompter.

'You can stick your little play. You'll have to amuse yourself without me.'

She goes back to the apartment, pulls a jumper and a raincoat on over her dress and goes out.

The gate of the Salinières stands alone in the middle of nowhere. An absurd, monumental portal, open on all sides to the defunct dock. L goes back to the quayside. A warm wind shunts dark clouds across the sky, revealing at intervals, in whole or in part, a dim, slightly dog-eared moon.

L walks along the river, too afraid to remain still watching it. There is a drawing of Hugues', in ink, sombre and naive, which shows the plan of the town split by the langorous arc of 'the Stream'. 'Can you see how it shines softly?' he said as he showed her the drawing. And he compared it to a silk stocking, stretched between the languid hips of the town. But I am suspicious of this river which washes a port smelling of wilting flowers, emptied of ships, haunted by empty warehouses and rusted rails.

L thinks that she must catch the plane and return home. She wonders whether she will ever be able to make the necessary effort. Get back to her normal life . . . How is it that she never noticed before this unbearable boredom which oozes from her life. But no, before she was happy. And now all of a sudden that happiness seems forbidden. Her former life now seems like a universe of innocence, a paradise lost. She feels overcome with nostalgia and expectation.

L crosses back over the quayside, follows the sinuous curve of the rue de la Rousselle, wanders aimlessly among the narrow streets of the old town. At the corner of the place Saint-Pierre she goes into a tiny bar with a tiled floor scattered with sawdust. There are only three tables and one customer, as old and ugly as the landlady.

L asks for a packet of cigarettes. The old woman with her unkempt grey hair carries on muttering to her customer as if she hasn't heard. L waits. Through the dirty window she notices the faded sign of a shop adjacent to the church: THE FATAL BODICE. In front of the lowered grill a young woman is peering into the window. Slim, dark-haired, a child's body in a small, old-fashioned white dress. Suddenly, L recognises Alice.

L is already through the door when a commanding voice calls her back.

'Your cigarettes!'

She hesitates for a moment, casts one last glance at the frail figure standing motionless on the other side of the square and comes back inside. Now she has a pain in her stomach, she is sweating. She sees as if in a dream the old woman dragging her heavy legs behind the counter and offering her the packet of cigarettes. L draws her hand slowly across her forehead, digs out her change, pays and leaves.

Gone. L stares at the spot where she saw her just a moment ago. With trembling legs she takes a few steps, then slumps down on the first bench, opposite the shop. She tries to get her breath back.

In front of the shop, at the spot where Alice stood just now, there is a sort of hole, a hole of darkness. L stands up and walks over to the spot, underneath the unlit sign. Behind the metal grill stands an armless woman with wide-open plastic eyes. A flesh-coloured satin bodice squeezes her wasp waist. At the back of the shop is a jumble of second-hand clothes, in the middle of which shimmers the yellow reflection of her hair.

In the ghostly glare of the spotlights the row of muses levitates above the deserted Grand Theatre. A young man in jeans and trainers, his shoulders bare in a red tank-top in spite of the cool evening, walks towards the building with a supple stride. With one hand he holds the multicoloured shoulder-strap of a large wooden drum with a feminine, hourglass shape. The young man stops on the first step of the theatre, places on the ground next to him a piece of African cloth folded into a square, hangs the heavy instrument from his shoulders and wedges it between his knees, and, still standing up, begins to beat the skin.

Rue des Faussets, a young woman in a white cotton dress pauses for a moment. Her heart is beating just as it did during the artist's most dangerous number in the circus a moment ago. Guided by the dull echo of the drum roll she goes quickly up the street, turns left into the rue du Puits-des-Cujols, right then left again, rue Saint-Rémi, now she is running, rue Jouannet, rue du Pont-de-la-Mosque, crosses the cours du Chapeau-Rouge. She slows down as she approaches the musician. She stops a few metres from him and listens, moving her body imperceptibly to the rhythm.

Now he has warmed up he beats harder and faster, varying the phrases with irregular pauses, his head thrown back. The skin has become warm as well, alive like a voice. And suddenly this voice begins to sing, a ghostly song from the depths of the wooden shell, as if the instrument itself had decided to accompany the musician.

The doors of the Grand Theatre open, releasing from its foyer of chandeliers and gilded decorations men and women in navy-blue raincoats, their eyes and ears still beribboned in the repetitive whirl of Viennese waltzes, swirling tutus and the old three-step refrains.

The musician carries on playing. The crowd pours down the steps, keeping a respectable distance on each side of him. One middle-aged woman, however, breaks the circle of taboo and drops a coin on the square of cloth, soon followed by one or two others. Then the steps empty. The musician finishes the phrase on one last variation. The young girl who has been standing apart all the way through comes up and speaks to him.

L is afraid. Alice may be here, in this town. L is afraid to remember. Alice, her dark angel. Alice who destroys through wanting to live too much.

The window reflects nothing of L but the yellow light of her hair; her face is nothing but a shapeless, blurred blob, submerged by shadow. Fatal bodies, says the sign, which says any old thing. Bodies know who kills. Behind the grill the pallid, plastic woman squints, her armless body inflates, the seams of the bodice split with a cracking sound, the satin rips from the breasts to the abdomen in a huge seismic fault. Cracks like lightning bolts run across her cheeks, her forehead, everything explodes, in one enormous breath everything explodes, hurling the shredded bodice against the window with jigsaw pieces of face, the white, globular eyes . . . Then the awful clothes piled up at the back of the shop drag themselves forward on their worn-out elbows, as if answering the call to some horrific feast.

'Do you fancy a drink?' asks Manu. 'I was playing at the Grand Theatre, I earned enough to buy a decent bottle.'

L enters the sitting-room with its dull wood panelling. Hugues and Mamadou are there. Sitting between them, Alice. She says simply: 'I was expecting you.' Alice squeezes up next to Hugues, to make space for her friend.

Mamadou gets up from the old sofa covered in an orange and yellow African cloth to sit on the floor, half stretched out on a cushion at Alice's feet.

'Music is tough, but life is great! Let's drink to that!'

Manu conscientiously rolls a joint, lights it and passes it round.

The glass of wine is already making her head spin. She sucks in the blend of warmth and softness, gives the joint to Alice, who takes two deep drags before passing it on to Hugues. Alice, looking like a childlike *femme fatale,* with her poor, badly cut, white dress, too cold for the time of year, her feet bare in her uncomfortable high-heeled shoes, and above all her sombre look, bright yet candid, which consumes her pale face, fringed with her long, very dark hair.

The hour is already late. Alice laughs, captivates everyone's gaze, dances alone in the middle of the room to the syncopated songs of Mamadou, casts the flame of her dark eyes all round, pours out at the top of her voice whatever comes into her head, sequences of unintelligible words, weird odds and ends of phrases. Where is my little sky cat? Oodles of spinning frogoodles, do you like noodles? I couldn't give a doodle, but the poor old sky has got a crick in his neck from leaning over him. Alice dances about, strange, mad. Drunk like she was at thirteen, without having drunk a single drop of wine. Alice who on stormy days never resisted the call of the wind, whom she saw from the bay windows of the school, walking round alone in the salty squalls, in the deserted yard, her arms open, head thrown back, illuminated, but disturbing, sometimes feeding the birds with crumbs of bread which were immediately whisked away by the gusts of wind. Alice floating for whole nights between floor and ceiling, perched uncomfortably on the narrow sill above the showers, watching the stars.

L remembers the night light falling through the fanlights on the white ceramic sinks, Alice suspended on high like that little statue of the angel which glowed when you took it under the sheets, which she would place at night on the cupboard between their two beds, where it gently illuminated their sleep. L remembers the tiredness which quickly caught up with her, forcing her to return to the dormitory, preventing her from following Alice on her long voyages across the night sky.

Still tightly wrapped in her raincoat, her head aching, L would like to go home, alone. Alice, suddenly gloomy, looks at Hugues like a jealous lover and says that she wants to see his paintings.

'Since you didn't come back to sit for me again,' says Hugues, 'I continued without you, from memory.' He has put on his architect's lamp, which casts its fierce light on the wall. The ink is incrusted in the paper like a tattoo. And yet the drawing seems to leap off the paper, such is the violence and vitality of the play of light and dark, accentuated by brushstrokes, sometimes thick and heavy, sometimes delicate like torn silk. The work is obviously incomplete. Some bits are still blank – ghostly spaces. One eye is merely sketched in while the other, heavily underlined, has a strangely deep, dark, brilliant gaze. The traces of wine on the insides of the thighs aren't there yet.

'It's not me,' she says.

'Be patient, it's not finished. I need you in order to finish it.'

'It's not me. The hair is too dark, the face is too pale, the body too slim, the eyes too gloomy. It's Alice.'

'It's you, Lucile. Sit for me again until morning, let me prove that it is you. This portrait means a lot to me, you know.'

Hugues is suddenly so tender, so pleading. L now knows that the straight, deserted road she has chosen must reach its end in this town. If you want to sleep you can have my bed, she tells Alice. This night she wants to spend alone with Hugues.

Alice looks at one then the other with the expression of a lost child, then in a single gesture pulls off her little white dress, throws it across the floor and goes and locks herself in the bathroom. There is a sharp grating noise as the taps are turned on, then the gurgling sound of the bath filling up.

L gets undressed, takes up her pose in the chair. Hugues prepares his inks and brushes, looks at her. He is just ready to start on the drawing when Alice starts calling out insistently for him from the bathroom.

Hugues opens the door and L sees a foot lifted out of the foam and dancing gently in the steam. She hears Alice murmur something. Hugues goes all the way in and closes the door behind him.

L remains motionless in the chair, waiting for Hugues to return.

She stretches out her arm to pick up the bottle of wine on the table. It is half full. She drains it deliberately in one go, drinking straight from the bottle.

There are only a few pieces left on the chess board, mainly black. The white queen is in check. L tries to work out how many moves are needed to win the game. It must be almost all over now. There is one thing which she doesn't understand about this solitary game. Given that Hugues is playing himself, he must simultaneously defend and attack both sides, each piece is both his friend and foe. Is it possible not to choose, to counter one's own tactics at each move, to outwit onself? L looks at the pieces, and suddenly the black knight comes to life and signals to her to come. L wants to cry out. She doesn't want to follow him, with his strange way of moving.

L turns away from the chess board. She feels colder than a statue. She curls up in the white sheet and turns in on herself.

Hugues doesn't return. In front of the bathroom there is a strip of marbled grey linoleum. A trickle of water worms its way under the door. Muffled gargling sounds echo off the walls of the apartment. The tongue of water, with its fringe of white foam, slowly spreads out.

A huge black cockroach darts out of a dark corner and stops right at the foot of the chair. L leans over, takes aim and crushes the insect with the base of the bottle. Its shell splits with a crack. A white pulp comes out, like the soft centre of a sweet. L lifts her arm again and hurls the bottle which breaks into large fragments on the floor. I knew it, Alice always has to destroy everything.

No one really knows what happened. I can do the talking, since she was already dead, I had already taken the whole space, there was nothing left for her but one last struggle like the blue tit; that hurt everyone, and everyone, especially me, would rather have avoided it, these painful moments, but it was already the end, and you can't skip the final convulsions, without them there's no deliverance. The problem is in knowing whether deliverance ever really comes. Life piles up corpses in our path. Living corpses or dead corpses, the bastards dig their nails into your flesh and rot your blood.

No one will really know what happened, because it is the liar who speaks. The one who doesn't believe in anything, the one who laughs, all the words dance at the masked ball, only the music is right. Do you like dancing, singing? There's nothing else to do, otherwise you're a vegetable. Not even that. The leek dances in the ground, with its happy little roots. And the carrot. It must be a bit frisky to get so crunchy! No, the walking corpses are men. Wandering souls fleeing death and life, dying of fear. L called me because she couldn't go on like that.

She opened the bathroom door and screamed. Hugues tried to hold her back, but she scratched his eyes and threw herself on me.

I felt myself being pulled violently by the hair. She was in a mad rage, she hurled me to the ground. Her naked body against mine, calling me slut, over and over. I started to cry and grabbed hold of her breasts which were swinging above me. Perhaps I said: mummy. Then she seemed exhausted, she collapsed onto me, and I cried a bit more into her hair. Then I untangled myself and she slumped like a rag doll between my hands. Crouching down, I kneaded her beautiful fleshy body, harder and harder, then I struck her, struck her all over with heavy slaps, as if trying to rouse her from a faint, and she wept and cried out and groaned with pain, and that gave me more and more pleasure.

Hugues pulled me by the shoulders to stop me doing this, and he tried to take her in his arms. She leaped up like a wounded animal, on all fours she began to scream, her face twisted by hate.

'Don't touch me! You filthy pig! Go and fuck her again, go fuck her like a pig!'

She was unrecognisable. Her neck stretched taut, the veins standing out, her pupils contracted, her features strained and distorted, frozen in the rictus of a woman possessed. She repeated: 'Go fuck her like a pig!' in a raucous, cavernous voice somewhere between a roar and a sob.

Hugues recoiled a little, then said to her, very calmly:

'Now you will listen to me. Nothing happened. Alice offered to tell me about you, about the time when you were friends. And that interested me. That's all. Can you understand that? If you don't believe me, ask her.'

Mamadou and Manu came up to find out what all the noise was about. They seemed really concerned, but Hugues explained that L was drunk, that he would take her out for a walk to calm her down, he convinced them that everything was fine.

While this was going on I went over to her and rubbed her stomach, like a baby, and she started crying again very softly. She was unhappy, my little sister, she talked to me in a low voice, she sounded as if she was frightened of me, as if she needed me. Tell me, you must know. Does he love me? He does? He does? I think I told her yes, he loved her, and I took her by the hand like we had done in the showers so that she would remember what she said, a single spirit in two bodies.

We were completely wet, we rolled ourselves up in a towel. Then I lent her my white dress and I put on her red dress. Mine was too tight on her, but I had never looked so beautiful. It was made of stretchy velvet, it moulded itself to me, gave me a shapely behind. I also put on the suspenders and stockings, I was mad with joy.

Hugues said he was going to take her for a walk by the river, to a spot where she would have the best view of the sky and the town. I looked at her, and she suggested I should come with them.

I take my bag, with the scissors inside, like my mother when she went out in the rain to leave us on the river bank. We get in the car and drive over the Pont-de-Pierre. The pitch-black Garonne glimmers. The ballet of headlamps and streetlamps turns the night into a yellow fairground. We hug the right bank for a short while, then Hugues parks the car on a grass verge. We go over a wooden footbridge, next to the foundations of a ruined building, and reach the landing-stage which juts out over the river.

We sit on the concrete slab which is cold and cracked. The river beneath our feet slowly swells its dark chest, as if troubled by bad dreams. All the lights of the town stretch out along the other bank, tangled strings of gold pearls.

The air is cool. Hugues wraps his arm around L to warm her up. I lie flat on my back to look at the sky. The clouds have nearly all cleared, but there is a sense that the stars are going to go out soon.

Hugues and L don't stop talking as they look at the water and the town. 'Nudity makes my head spin,' he says. 'Like the void. I need to disguise the world in order to bear it, to transform it. You are the first woman I have drawn completely nude, that's why things have been so difficult between us. It's as if I was afraid of you.'

Then they are silent. They appear to kiss. I get up and walk to the edge of the slab, taking care not to fall into the black holes which twice loom up in front of me. There is a rusty iron ladder embedded in the concrete. I climb down to the river bank.

I sit down in the damp grass. I wait. The water of the night is full of silent eddies, like those of the stars in the fluctuating sky.

During the day I stayed by my window, listening to the leaves. Brown and black birds skipped in the grass, stopping with their heads held stiff, eyes on the lookout, then plunging their little beaks into the ground and withdrawing them quickly, quivering through their entire bodies. In this way, with short hops, they worked their way through the whole space, the whole day. Sometimes a cat, which I later got to know, watched them from the trees. He could remain motionless for ever. The shadows lengthened as the hours passed, the air carried softer, more penetrating smells. It was the evening for everything, when you slept awake. The mauve flowers on the balcony closed and I never saw them move.

*

When I looked at the garden from my bed, framed in its rectangle of daylight, I entered without entering the quivering green of the willows and the lawn, where my body became transparent, run through with rootlets. It was a very luminous picture because of the pearls of silver dripping from the sun onto the back of every leaf and every blade of grass. It was terrifyingly sweet to behold it, to become part of it like an internal, nourishing spring in this sea-green flood of vegetation. The park asked nothing of me; it called me constantly with its secret mouth: mud of blue sky and yellow earth.

When I see the man I am so enraptured by his beauty, his eyes, his strength, I feel like crying. Crying because of those who will have neglected me when I desired them, because of those who loved me when it was impossible.

I will never again hear the wind rustling in the willows, never again see them twisting their thousands of loving arms. And he with whom I will fall endlessly, totally in love, I will never hold him, dearest love, I can no more hold you than the much lamented wind of the trees.

*

The dampness of the river has penetrated my dress. The stars have all gone, it is nearly day now. I climb back up the rusty ladder to the landing-stage. Hugues and L are still there. I pick up a loose lump of concrete and walk towards them.

The sky is already growing pale, they will miss the dawn. They are busy making love, they don't hear me approach. They are fully dressed. They are looking at each other as if they wanted to see deep into the other's entrails. Then she arches back violently, she is going to moan and cry out, I can't wait any longer. The lump of concrete is hurting me, it is too heavy. I raise my arms a little and drop it on her head.

She and Hugues do not turn away from each other. They stop moving, but continue to look at each other as if it were the last thing left for them to do, as if they had something pressing to say to each other. Then her eyes suddenly show nothing. Hugues finally looks at the red hole in her temple and the trickles of blood running through her blond hair.

I think Hugues wanted to kill me at first, but almost immediately he broke down like a child and lay next to her, crying. Finally he went off, saying that he would be back. I heard the car start.

The night has finished tearing itself apart. Pink and yellow clouds stretch out across the pale sky, long and thin like branches. I close my eyes. I take my scissors out of my bag, I raise her head slightly and I cut her hair back to her neck. The scissors rasp and gleam. L is beautiful, pale as the fleeting dawn in her white dress.

I sit down on the edge of the landing-stage. Above the river, in front of a nearby wooden hut, there are nets hanging on posts. In the hesitant daylight the water is sea-green, almost muddy. I throw in the hair.

No one will know what really happened, because no one can get outside themselves to understand really what takes place. Perhaps L left in the car with Hugues, in love. She has laid her head on his shoulder, she smiles, the road unfurls in the early morning. Perhaps L never came back to this town. Perhaps I am the one who died, bloated by the water of 'the Stream'.

*

A fisherman rows upstream. I wave to him, I call him, finally he rows over to the bank. Perhaps L remained lying in the ditch, perhaps I played at being L. I go down to the riverbank, he lands, I climb on board, we row back into the middle of the river. The blond hair dances like luminous algae in our wake, then drifts away.